Rescuing Einstein's Compass

For my family, with love – SLO
For future scientists – GJ

First published in 2003 by
CROCODILE BOOKS
An imprint of Interlink Publishing Group, Inc.
46 Crosby street, Northampton, Massachusetts 01060
www.interlinkbooks.com

Book design by George Juhasz ~ Illustrations scanned by ScanLab ~ Pre-press U&I Type Services Ltd.

Library of Congress Cataloging-in-Publication Data

Oppenheim, Shulamith Levey.
Rescuing Einstein's Compass / by Shulamith Levey Oppenheim
p. cm.
Summary: Eight-year-old Theo takes the famous scientist, Albert Einstein, sailing on the lake and rescues his compass when it falls into the water.
ISBN 1-56656-507-3
1. Einstein, Albert, 1879-1955 – Juvenile fiction.
[1. Einstein, Albert, 1879-1955 – Fiction. 2. Compass – Fiction 3. Sailing – Fiction.]
I. Title.
PZ7.0618 Re 2003
[E] dc21
2002151100

Printed and bound in Korea

To request our complete 48-page full-color catalog, please call us toll free at 1-800-238-LINK, visit our website at www.interlinkbooks.com, or write to
Interlink Publishing
46 Crosby Street, Northampton, MA 01060-1804
E-mail: info@interlinkbooks.com

Rescuing Einstein's Compass

By Shulamith Levey Oppenheim ∽ Illustrated by George Juhasz

Crocodile Books, USA
An imprint of Interlink Publishing Group, Inc.
New York • Northampton

If you are lucky, something happens in your life that you never forget...something so special you know it could happen only to you. For Theo, that something happened the day he rescued Albert Einstein's compass.

It was on a Sunday morning. As Theo came down the stairs, he heard violin music coming from the living room. Papa and Mama were waiting for him in the hallway.

Papa said to him, "Today, Theo, we have a great treat for you. Today you are going to meet the most famous man alive."

The most famous man alive! Theo couldn't imagine who it could be. "What is his name?" Theo asked. "I already know my two grandfathers."

"Albert Einstein," Mama answered, as she straightened Theo's jacket.

"Albert!" Theo tried not to laugh. "My friend Karl has a new puppy named Albert."

"Theo!" Papa raised a finger, as he always did when he was going to say something very important. "You must call him Herr Professor Einstein. He is a physicist."

Now Theo was a curious boy, so he asked, "Why is he the most famous man alive, Papa? What does a physicist do?"

He smiled. "You may ask the Herr Professor those questions," he answered.

Theo took Mama's hand. "I'm afraid, Mama." She squeezed his fingers. "Papa has never before called anyone the most famous man alive."

Papa took Theo's other hand and said, "Come, come, Theo. You are eight years old. Our guest does not bite!"

As they neared the living room, Theo heard a deep chuckle. "*Nooooo,* Einstein does not bite. Your father and I have been close friends for many years. He would know by now if I did," said the Herr Professor, as he chuckled even louder.

Theo looked up. The man had a thick black moustache and a large head with gray-black hair bushing out all over it. His eyes were dark and merry, but Theo still felt nervous.

"Now, young man, let us get immediately to business. Your parents tell me that you have a sailboat. I have loved sailing since I was your age. Will you take me out in your boat? It is a beautiful day."

Theo looked at his parents. Take the most famous man alive in his little sailboat! Theo's neck and cheeks felt hot. His tongue felt thick and furry.

Mama and Papa nodded. “That’s right, Theo.” Mama looked very pleased. “Our guest is an experienced sailor. We thought it would be lovely for the two of you to go out on the lake.”

Mama and Papa waved from the doorstep.

“Let us be off!” bellowed the most famous man alive, as he put a hand on Theo’s shoulder.

Theo and Herr Professor Einstein walked down the hill and through a line of giant blue spruce trees that edged the lake. "Is there always so much bird song here, Theo?" the professor asked. "It is *wunderbahr* to have the air filled with such sounds. Wonderful!"

"It's spring, and they're laying their eggs in the nests they've built in these trees," Theo answered. His tongue was finally unstuck and his legs didn't feel quite like jelly. "They're happy. Do you have birds at your house?"

"No, no." Einstein smiled at Theo. "Not now. I live in the city. But when I was a boy and went sailing on a lake near my home, there were birds everywhere. What have you named your boat?"

"*Fleet Felix*," Theo answered proudly.

Herr Professor Einstein grinned. "I like that. And where exactly is *Fleet Felix* moored?"

Theo pointed to a pier that was just coming into view. A bright green boat was rocking gently on the water.

FLEET FELIX

FELIX

The Herr Professor untied the rope from the mooring, coiled it up, and tossed it on the boat. They climbed aboard. Once they raised the sail, Theo took the tiller and the professor held the sheet. They were off! There was a light breeze. The clouds were white cotton puffs and the sky seemed as blue to Theo as his Mama's eyes.

Theo decided this was a fine moment to ask his questions. He took a deep breath.

"Yes?" Professor Einstein asked. How did the Herr Professor know he was going to ask a question, Theo wondered.

"Why are you the most famous man alive and what does a physicist do?"

Einstein didn't answer right away. He put his hand into his pocket. "Hmm... it has fallen through a hole in the lining," he muttered. Then the most famous man alive threw back his great head and laughed and laughed. Theo was glad to see him laugh, but he didn't understand.

"What has fallen through a hole in your pocket?" Theo asked, as politely as he could.

"Something that will help explain what a physicist does. *Himmel*!" boomed out the Professor.

"Heavens! I think it is somewhere under the pocket, now.... One minute, one minute, I must tear the lining...a little more, a little more.... There, now! I shall fish it out, only it won't be a fish but..."

By this time Theo was laughing, too. The professor drew out his hand. Between his fingers was—a compass!

"Bravo!" Herr Professor shouted. "Now I'll tell you a story." Theo looked up at the sky. Two hawks were riding the warm currents, or the thermals, as Papa called them. *Fleet Felix* was catching the breeze perfectly. Herr Professor Einstein's voice was very low now.

"When I was five years old I was quite ill. I had to stay in bed for many days. My father gave me this compass. You know what a compass is for, Theo?"

Theo nodded.

"Good," Herr Professor continued. "It was the first compass I had ever seen. There was the needle, under glass, all alone, pointing north no matter which way I turned the compass. It seemed like magic. Only it wasn't magic at all. Do you know why?"

Theo took a very deep breath. "Because the needle is magnetic, and there is a magnet at the North Pole that attracts the needle?"

Herr Professor raised his bushy eyebrows. "*Nearly* correct. There are two magnetic poles, north and south. So far away! And there, in my bedroom, on the palm of my hand, was my compass, always pointing north. For me, a boy of five, this was the greatest mystery I could imagine. And so I decided then and there that I would learn all about the forces in the world that we cannot see. For I certainly could not..."

At that moment a large motorboat zoomed past them, stirring up the water into high waves. One of the waves hit *Fleet Felix* against the side. Herr Professor lost his balance, and the compass fell from his hand right into the water!

He stared at his empty palm. "The compass, Theo, it is gone! Overboard?" Suddenly Theo saw sadness in the professor's eyes. "I should hate to lose it. And I cannot swim very well… and my eyes…" His voice trailed off, and he seemed to be looking far into space.

Theo knew what he had to do! He dropped the anchor and took off his shoes. Then he jumped into the water.

Papa and Mama had always said Theo must have been a fish before he was a boy. Now he had a chance to prove it.

First, he swam around and around the boat. Then he dove under, searching beneath the hull as long as he could hold his breath. Then he came up and swam around to the bow where his friend was sitting with his eyes closed! He made two rounds—three, four... but still there was no compass!

He had to find it! Herr Professor Einstein might be the most famous man alive right now, but once he had been a little boy and his father had given him a compass that he loved.

Theo thought about the book of poems with beautiful engravings that his own parents had given him and how he would feel if he lost it. He made another dive under the boat. Just as he came up for air, he felt something hit his cheek. It was the compass, bobbing alongside *Fleet Felix*, just waiting to be rescued!

Grabbing the compass in one hand, Theo hoisted himself up into the boat with the other. Herr Professor Einstein looked as if he were asleep.

"Pardon me," Theo called to him. "Pardon me, Herr Professor Einstein, here is your compass!"

Einstein opened his eyes. "So," he smiled at Theo, "this is what a physicist does...." The professor continued talking just as if nothing had happened. "A physicist studies the forces in nature that we cannot see directly, only we know that they are there from what we observe, like the compass needle or..."

"Or gravity!" Theo added, very excited to have remembered this.

"Bravo, young man. Like gravity! All these forces keep our planet running quite smoothly most of the time. And thank you, dear Theo. For me, you are the most famous boy alive!"

The professor's eyes were merry again. Theo was still trying to catch his breath, but he had to ask his other question. "Was it because of the compass that you are the most famous man alive?"

Theo's new friend sat very still. "The compass was my first mystery and all my life I have worked to solve mysteries. And—" he put the compass in his pocket, the same one with the hole in it—"I am not the most famous man alive, no matter what your dear father thinks. But you are certainly the bravest and kindest boy I know!"

FELIX

When the two sailors got back to the house, Mama asked Theo why he was soaked.

"We had an adventure," answered Herr Professor Einstein, "one I don't think either of us shall ever forget!"

That night Theo wondered what Papa and Mama would say if they knew that the most famous man alive couldn't swim very well—and had a hole in his pocket.

Author's Note

My husband was a young boy when he first met Albert Einstein. His father did introduce Professor Einstein to him as "the most famous man alive." And Einstein had been given a compass by his father when he was five years old and sick in bed. The rest of this story is fiction.

Einstein was the best man at our wedding. During the ceremony, the ring dropped through a hole in Einstein's pocket. He stared straight ahead without a blink, not moving a muscle, while it was fished out!

Einstein was often called a man beyond time and space, yet at the same time he was very down-to-earth. He played the violin. He rode his bicycle to the Institute for Advanced Study in Princeton, New Jersey, which was founded for him. He loved jokes. Sometimes he laughed so hard while telling a joke we never heard the punch line! He had a small dog who, Einstein assured everyone, was the source of all knowledge.

Einstein's backyard was a haven for birds. He would sit in the garden for hours while his stepdaughter, Margot, talked to them.

Einstein gave us an over-arching explanation for the workings of those hidden forces in the universe. He helped people understand the relationship between time and space. His theory of relativity revolutionized physics, and it has enabled scientists who have come after him to make discoveries and derive explanations from their experiments that might not otherwise have been possible.